C. S. JOHNSON

NIGHT

of

BLOOD and BEAUTY

A COMPANION NOVELLA TO

THE ORDER OF THE CRYSTAL DAGGERS

◊   ◊   ◊   ◊

C. S. Johnson

1st Edition.
eBook ISBN: 978-1-948464-25-3
Paperback ISBN: 978-1-948464-26-0

This book is first dedicated, as nearly always—at least so much that it's strange, especially if you don't see it with the spirit of my intent—to Sam.

But it is also dedicated to my good friends, Jennifer, Cathy, and Laura, whose support and enthusiasm helped bring this story into being, if for no other reason than their insistence made it so.

To Get *Awakening* (A Special Christmas Episode of The *Starlight Chronicles*) as a bonus for picking up this book,

Click Here

Or Download It At:
https://www.csjohnson.me/awakening

1

◊

"Miss Eleanor."

The desperation in his voice was only matched by his irritation, and the moment he said anything, Amir feared he had inadvertently given himself away.

The sapphire eyes he had come to both love and hate twinkled mischievously at him. "Why, Mr. Qureshi, I do believe you're quite flustered. Especially if you're going to use your manners. Where are those mongrel ways of yours? I might mistake you for a real gentleman with such a formal tone."

Her lyrical, teasing voice did nothing to lighten his mood; rather, it plucked at his heartstrings with a bittersweet twang, and Amir had to force himself to remain still as he stared down at her.

It would do nothing for his case if he showed any further sign of compromise, especially now that his partner sensed his weakness.

"It is only proper I address you as such, Miss Eleanor," Amir said, keeping his voice stripped of all his conflicting emotions. "Your mother, Her Grace, would be the first to agree with me."

At the mention of her mother, her gaze only grew bolder. "We both know my mother's favorite thing in the world is being a hypocrite," she said, crossing her arms and tapping her toe. "Call me Naděžda, as I've told you to before several times now."

Inwardly, Amir groaned. He should have known better than to say anything. If there was anything Eleanor Naděžda Ollerton-Cerná excelled at—and there was plenty—it was

1

THE ORDER OF THE CRYSTAL DAGGERS

arguing with him. And while there was enough wrong with that in itself, it unnerved him how often he found himself losing those arguments.

"Miss Eleanor, propriety demands—"

"Is this my punishment, after all these years, to have you give me the same lecture I gave you when we first met, Amir?" Naděžda asked, arching her brow as she pouted.

Amir hated how he stared at her mouth. His Abba had always been so concerned about him looking into a woman's eyes that Amir never realized how sinful looking at a woman's lips could be. Even beneath her *yashmak*, the transparent veil worn by women on the streets of Constantinople, seeing Naděžda stick out her bottom lip was like watching a rose bloom under misty moonlight.

He was secretly relieved when she crossed her arms and let out an indignant sigh, turning her face to the side; her patience was dwindling as quickly as his resolve.

All I have to do is outlast her. Amir relaxed in the slightest degree; it was always easier to outlast her than it was to outwit her.

"If I didn't know you better, I would question your intellect," she said.

"What is stopping you? You've questioned it often enough in the past several months we've been working together on the Order's missions." Amir frowned, his own patience wearing thin. "Unless, of course, you have good reason to agree with me in this case?"

"I fail to see why finding a way to engage the target would be a mistake. He's old enough to be more patient with someone of my age."

"He's old enough to see you as a nuisance."

2

"Doubtful. He's likely no more than ten years older than I am, probably married with a wife and an heir at home. A little flirtation from someone like me will make him feel like a young, attractive, appreciated hero. We've followed him long enough to know he's a soft touch."

Amir frowned. "Now I really don't like your idea. He could fall in love with you on sight."

"What better way to get him to slip up?" Naděžda sneered. "If anything can ruin your life, it is love."

He hated both her tone and how much he agreed with her. "Spies are not supposed to fall in love."

Though his tone did not betray it, that reminder was one that was burned into him daily, often multiple times as he worked with Naděžda.

She was a member of the Order of the Crystal Daggers, an ancient group of spies and assassins, specializing in political security and clandestine reconnaissance missions. Naděžda's mother was its leader, and Lady Penelope took great pride in her responsibilities, with an unrivaled, orderly fervor. While their adventures varied in location, task, and time, Amir always embraced the chance to work beside Naděžda. While he was not a member of the Order, he was a medical adviser and companion on many of their assignments.

Above all else, he sought to honor that trust. That was why he had to keep Naděžda safe—perhaps despite her wishes otherwise on such matters.

Amir cleared his throat cautiously. "Right now, it would be an unnecessary complication, especially if you are right about the wife and nursery at home."

"But it would be so easy." She clasped her hands together. "He's drawn to books. What better way to get his attention and earn his respect than engaging him at the book vendor?"

3

THE ORDER OF THE CRYSTAL DAGGERS

"No matter how much he loves books and no matter how much charm you throw his way, the Bohemian ambassador is not going to discuss business with the likes of you."

Amir glanced back at their target. They had been following him for hours now, ever since he walked through the construction site where the sultan's new Dolmabahçe Palace was being built.

Considering the crowded streets of Constantinople, and the finer points of the Bohemian's diplomacy, finding him was a miracle more than anything else. Amir did not want to lose him, and Amir especially did not want to lose him because he was too distracted from arguing with Naděžda.

And over such nonsense, too.

"I should go anyway," Naděžda murmured behind him, just loudly enough he knew she was angry enough to be serious. "You never let me do what I want."

"That's enough," Amir told her sharply. "The ambassador is the one who is supposed to meet with the merchants from the Haberecht Shipping Company, and we need to find out where they are located and why he is meeting with them. Her Grace says the company has rebellious sympathies. She suspects they could be behind the missing shipment themselves, rather than the Ottomans who supposedly took off with it."

"King Ferdinand is not concerned about the rebels. He just wants the weapons for himself."

"A king is allowed to protect his own country."

"Yes, but how can he protect himself from his own country? There is trouble brewing in Bohemia, just as there is trouble in Italy, Germany, and other Austrian principalities."

"That is why we need to find out where the shipment went."

4

Naděžda wrinkled her nose. "My father would likely know. If we really wanted to find out, all we would have to do is ask him."

"You know how Her Grace feels about that," Amir said quietly.

"She probably thinks he is behind it, given his own history with the League of Ungentlemanly Warfare. That's likely the main reason the Order is here, isn't it? There is nothing my mother would love more than to strike out against my father, especially now that she has the full weight of the British Empire behind her as a League member herself."

"Even if he's not behind it, we need to find the truth. Those weapons could unwittingly cause a lot of trouble for the people, even if they are the ones who end up wielding them."

"I suppose that is true," Naděžda agreed, her voice full of sad resignation.

Amir fell silent. He did not know what to say, especially since, from what he knew, Naděžda was likely correct. Ever since her parents' tumultuous affair and failed partnership, there was nothing but enmity in Lady Penelope's eyes at the mention of him.

Naděžda sighed. Seeing the soft vulnerability in her features made Amir want to reach out and comfort her.

Instead, Amir turned away, allowing her privacy while she grappled with her family's brokenness. A long moment passed in silence between them, before Naděžda sighed.

Amir took it as a sign she was ready to move on. "Right now, we just need to find the actual destination of the shipment."

"It could have been easily dispensed on the black markets already."

"That's true, but you said it yourself. This is something that is tied to the unrest in different countries, and we need to be prepared if fighting breaks out."

"Yes."

"So we need to follow the ambassador now, not flirt with him."

Naděžda whipped out a small fan from underneath the embroidered shawl she carried, fluttering it playfully in front of her half-covered face. "Well, my dear, you wouldn't be the one flirting, would you?" She straightened herself, drawing herself up to her full height, just shy of meeting him at eye level. "That is my area of expertise."

"You needn't remind me." The words came out softer much more husky, more provocative than he had intended. There was a quick, fearful gleam in her eye, and he saw she was uncomfortable, too.

She quickly played it off, snapping her fan shut and brushing off the billowing folds of her striped walking gown.

"Goodness, do all the women in this town have to be so covered up? I'm dying in these multiple layers," she said.

"The privacy of women is sacred here," Amir reminded her, more than grateful for the change in topic. "When something is sacred, it becomes law, and as such, modesty is the law of the land."

"There is no tyrant quite like one in place for one's own good, is there?"

"You should appreciate it. Wasn't your mother in Her Majesty Queen Victoria's court this past month?" Amir could not resist provoking her. "And even now you're wearing the bustle that's *à la mode*, and that seems much more troublesome than a veil."

The large, bulbous bump at the back of her gown twitched as Naděžda huffed.

"I might as well wear the Western fashions. I'm not going to blend in here," Naděžda insisted. "Even with the veil."

She was right about that, Amir thought to himself. In all the years since he had known her, she had never fit into any aspect of his life comfortably. Being so close to his childhood home, he was disheartened to see she never would.

He studied Naděžda out of the corner of his eye as she stood next to him in the small, dark corner of an alleyway. They were just outside the Court of the Mosque of Sultan Ahmed I, where tents poured out into the middle of the crowded streets and shops were tucked away behind them. The bright wooden buildings bordering the streets were interspersed with lattice-covered windows, hinting at the private sitting rooms afforded to women, allowing them a safe escape from the surrounding world of men and their markets.

Yes, Amir thought, Naděžda was indeed out of place. But knowing her as he did, he also knew she was accustomed to the experience.

"It's so hot." Naděžda waved her fan distractedly. "I'll be lucky if I don't die out here."

"You get used to the dry heat after a time," Amir told her. "And it is not all bad. It allows you to taste the salt in the air from the Bosporus, once you're close enough to the harbor, and you feel the full blessing of Allah from the wind."

"You could also assume that the heat was flying up from hell itself," Naděžda murmured, and despite his better judgment, Amir smiled.

Not one of his family members would approve of Naděžda in the slightest. She was everything he had been taught to abhor in a woman—outspoken, brash, impatient, stubborn,

7

and at times domineering. She had an enormous awareness of propriety, if only because she learned how to break it so beautifully. Many times they had fought, on everything from customs to food to manners, to religion and politics and family.

Given his own upbringing, he should have hated it. But Naděžda was smart and passionate, and he almost always enjoyed fighting with her just to see that spark of challenge light up her eyes.

Almost always.

"As I see it, the faster we get the information we need, the sooner we can head back to the ship and report back to Uncle," she said, gathering her skirts. "Talking with the ambassador would save us time."

"Mr. Prasad would not approve of your methods," Amir countered, thinking of his mentor and sponsor.

If there was ever a man he was indebted to, it was Harshad Prasad, and he would not see Naděžda come to ruin for anything. Part of the reason Harshad insisted they work together was so Amir could protect her. With the medical training he had received as a doctor, both from his father and Harshad's patronage, and having the benefits of understanding Western and Eastern cultures, he was more than capable of seeing to Naděžda's safety as she worked for the Order of the Crystal Daggers, especially in places such as Constantinople.

In theory, anyway.

Naděžda pursed her lips, reminding Amir of her mother, and he groaned. The newly proclaimed leader of the Order, Lady Penelope Ollerton-Wellesley, the dowager duchess of Wellington, was a force of nature, and she had taught her daughter to wield chaos just as skillfully than she did, if not more so.

Queen Victoria was no doubt very fortunate to have Lady Penelope's loyalty, Amir thought. The Order of the Crystal Daggers was an ancient society, one that was originally established to protect and maintain peace in Constantine's empire. When the Empire fell, the Order remained, quickly aligning themselves with those who were able to protect and assist them.

Which is why Harshad was here, Amir recalled. They had arrived with Harshad on the *Splendor*, one of the teak clippers from the East India Company. As an honorary member of the League of Ungentlemanly Warfare, Harshad was overseeing the fulfillment of the Treaty of Nanking, ensuring Chinese were complying with the terms of their loss. He would report back to Queen Victoria and the House of Lords when they returned to London.

It was fortunate Harshad was here, too, or they might never have realized a shipment of weapons intended to go to Prague had gone missing, or that the Bohemian ambassador had arrived for unexpected meetings with the Sultan and the Haberecht Shipping Company.

Naděžda cleared her throat, drawing Amir back to the moment.

"Are you sure it's Uncle who would not approve of my idea, Mr. Qureshi, or is it just you? Because I do believe Ambassador Svoboda would approve of me, and his approval is more important."

"What are you saying?"

Naděžda leaned toward him, batting her eyelashes flirtatiously. "I do believe you're jealous."

"Why would I be jealous?" Amir frowned, suddenly defensive. "This has nothing to do with that."

"Is that so?"

THE ORDER OF THE CRYSTAL DAGGERS

"Yes, and it never would," Amir insisted. He immediately regretted the sharpness in his voice.

Naděžda smiled bitterly, her eyes suddenly much sharper than before. "Well, then, as long as you have no claim on me, I'm overruling your order, Amir, with the stern reminder I am here as your partner, not your associate and certainly not your underling." She flipped her shawl over her shoulder proudly. "If anything, you are here under *my* seniority, given that I am the one in the Order, and you are merely here at Uncle's wishes."

"Miss Eleanor." This time, his voice came out as a hiss, but it was too late. She feinted and sidestepped him, before bustling out into the sunlight of the street, where the bazaar was full of mid-morning shoppers.

2

◊

As Naděžda coyishly dabbled from vendor to vendor, Amir wondered if time had slowed merely to torment him. A woman's privacy was sacred among the streets of Constantinople, but he knew, much more than he wanted to, that the harems and concubines of the Turkish court were full of Western fashions, and as much as Naděžda might have adopted the *yashmak* to soften her charm, he had a feeling it would only enhance her appeal. He watched as she alternatively enchanted and horrified various sellers with her confident demeanor.

She could be in danger.

His hand closed around the *Wahabite Jambiya* at his side, the curved dagger his father had passed onto him before he had set out for the Western universities.

"For your protection, and the blessing of the family," his Abba had said, and Amir was more than thankful that in all his years abroad, and even during the past months working alongside Naděžda, he had never needed to use it to protect himself.

He was a doctor, after all. He worked to preserve life, not take it away.

"*Pardonnez-moi, madame.*" Naděžda's voice cut through his musings, and Amir sneaked a glance at her as she questioned a flower-seller over the different blossoms she had available.

Amir frowned, watching as Naděžda handed over her payment, recognizing his coin purse in her hand. He groaned, realizing she must have grabbed it when she had dashed past him.

11

"*Merci beaucoup, au revoir.*" Naděžda gave a little curtsey to the flower-seller, her arms now carrying a slightly wilting bouquet of crocus, and the gypsy woman seemed to stand much more proudly as she waved farewell to her customer. Amir did not have to ask to know she had paid full price for the flowers.

She glanced over her shoulder, pretending to adjust her veil as she winked at him.

Amir frowned in reply, but the instant she turned away, he gave her a reluctant smile. He might have hated how well she worked, but watching her do so was a thing of beauty.

He lost his grin the instant he saw her duck behind the Bohemian Ambassador, who was looking through a line of books at another vendor.

Naděžda shifted her bustle, bumping into him. The ambassador turned around, and Naděžda followed suit, smoothly enough his arm collided with hers, and her newly-purchased flowers scattered to the ground.

"Oh, dear," she said, switching to her natural Bohemian accent. "My flowers."

Amir winced. While she never said it explicitly, she hated to indulge in anything that reminded her of her father. Amir did not know the whole story of her life there, before Lady Penelope's abrupt, troublesome departure from Naděžda's father. But while she seemed to loathe the very mention of it, he had seen the light in her eyes many times when she spoke of Bohemia, and when they were alone, as they were, she always insisted upon him using her Bohemian name, even if it was against social convention.

As the man began to apologize profusely to Naděžda, Amir turned to study him, grateful for the chance for a closer look. While there was nothing wrong with him in appearance—he was clearly a man in his thirties, one who was well-read despite coming from humble means—there was something about him that Amir did not like. There were rough sores on his hands and while he had made little attempt to tame the longer locks of his coal-colored hair, his mustache seemed too trim for the streets of Constantinople.

Perhaps that was it, Amir admitted to himself. The man was a stranger here, too, and that was something Naděžda would use to her advantage—and possibly something the ambassador could use to his, if she let him.

Amir hated him for that.

He watched as Ambassador Svoboda finally finished stuttering out his speech. The man seemed to be an odd choice for a diplomat; his words came awkwardly off his tongue, as if he never said anything more than he had to.

Amir huffed disgruntledly, wondering if it was Naděžda's charm. She looked distressed and her eyes brimmed with tears—those lovely, sapphire seas—until the poor man insisted that he replace her flowers.

Naděžda skillfully slipped down her veil as she dabbed at her small tears with a handkerchief before adjusting it back into place. Amir frowned as the man did not bother to duck his head, watching as the man's face lit up with wonder.

Amir stepped closer, preparing himself to pull Naděžda away from him, inching close enough to hear their conversation.

"I assure you, Madame—"

"Please, sir, it is Miss." Her eyelashes fluttered up at him again. "It is Miss Cerná."

"Oh. Oh, I see. Yes, I assure you, Miss Cerná, you have my humblest apologies," he said. "I will replace your flowers, and if you will let me, I will do so ten times over."

"Oh, you are too much, sir." She pulled out her fan and touched it to her veiled lips thoughtfully. "What a true gentleman you are."

Amir sighed quietly. Only Naděžda could go from a damsel in distress to a smoldering temptress before turning into a shy tease within three sentences.

"Please, Miss Cerná," the man said. "Allow me to formally introduce myself. I am Adolf Svoboda, an ambassador to His Imperial Majesty, King Ferdinand V of Bohemia—though perhaps you might also know him as Emperor Ferdinand I of the Austria-Hungarian Empire."

"I was wondering if you were from Bohemia like myself," Naděžda said, her voice full of sudden excitement. "And you say you are a member of the king's court? Why, how fascinating."

Amir forced himself not to grumble as Naděžda chatted with him, apologizing for her overly suggestive remarks with the youthful, innocent naivety that never failed to make men look twice as she wound a colorful, woeful tale of getting separated from her guard and in desperate need of assistance.

The ambassador, for his part, was fully under her spell, not even thinking to question her at all, nor even considering his own plans—at least, not until he realized he had not purchased his book.

"Excuse me one moment, Miss Cerná," he said, placing his hand over hers gently. "I will pay for this book, and then I will assist you in finding your guard. I know the women in Constantinople are largely left alone, but I shudder to think of you lost on the streets here."

"Of course, sir. Why, I am surprised I forgot, but I wished to buy a book myself."

Amir crossed his arms, pretending to study the carpets on the display before him. He had been wondering if that was

14

Naděžda's true aim all along. He was not surprised to hear the ambassador offer to buy her a book of her choice.

"As part of my apologies for your flowers, Miss Cerná, please allow me to purchase one for you," he said, before waving his arm over the long spread of books before him.

"Oh, I could not impose, sir—"

"Nonsense, I insist."

"Well, if you insist," Naděžda replied, with just enough humility and resignation to make it sound as though she had absolutely no choice in the matter. Amir recognized it as the same voice she would use in accepting her missions for the Order, even if he knew she hated it.

He had a feeling in this case, she did not hate it at all.

It was not long before she picked one up. "How about this one?" she asked, turning back to the ambassador to look for his approval.

The searching look in her eye suddenly made Amir want to give up the charade, march over to her and haul her over his shoulder, before taking her back to their ship and paying off the captain to leave early, their mission be damned.

She never looked at him for approval like that, Amir thought bitterly. His fist tightened around the curved dagger at his side, his fingers brushing over the calligraphic inscriptions in search of comfort.

He did not find any, and he found even less when he realized Naděžda was more likely to deride his opinions in such matters. Amir remembered how appalled she was upon hearing he had never read any Shakespeare the other night, and suddenly wondered if she was purchasing the book for him.

Amir glanced back as the ambassador looked over her choice.

15

"I commend you on your choice, Miss Cerná," he said. "I have read several of Wordsworth's works as well."

Amir felt his heart sink.

"I've heard that *The Prelude* is a lovely preface to reading any Shakespeare," Naděžda replied.

"I thought that as well," the ambassador agreed, looking through her book. While he talked on some of the content at length, Naděžda shot Amir a triumphant look over her shoulder, and he felt a little better.

"What did you choose, sir, if you don't mind my asking?" Naděžda clutched the book he'd handed back to her, sneaking a peek at his own choice.

"One of Percy Shelley's works," Adolf replied, suddenly eager to talk of his love for the romantics and their style, and other things that Amir did not know of. It seemed that the man had a deep interest in books, philosophy and art, and Amir had to commend Naděžda on her luck as well as her skill; this was a target she would enjoy talking with, rather than any number of their previous informants.

Naděžda kept the ambassador in good company while Amir followed at a distance.

As the time passed, Amir started to get impatient, and he was tempted to hate the Bohemian ambassador more and more—and maybe even Naděžda, too. She clung to the man's arm more tightly than necessary, giving the illusion she was his wife far more than a grateful stranger who believed he was doing her a favor.

It was only when the *Asr* call to prayer sounded down from the mosques in the city that the ambassador seemed to wake from Naděžda's spell.

"Goodness, look at the time," he exclaimed. "I have a meeting down by the Bosporus."

THE ORDER OF THE CRYSTAL DAGGERS

"Oh, dear," Naděžda said. "I have not inconvenienced you too long, have I?"

"I will find a way to send word to him, my dear Miss Cerná," Adolf promised. "We must find your guard. Your safety is much more of a concern than my business meeting."

"Oh, well, if you are certain." Naděžda pulled out her fan again. "Where did you say your meeting was? Perhaps, if we walked toward it, we will find someone who can help me locate my guard, too."

"My meeting is down at Marmora Pier, and I regret to say, Miss Cerná, that the docks are all about business, and there is no place for a lady such as yourself to be there. Perhaps I can find you some accommodation?"

It was at that, Amir decided he'd had enough, and it was time to make his entrance. He took out his weapon and held it at the ready as he stepped forward.

"Miss Cerná," he called, purposefully thickening his Turkish accent.

At his greeting, the Bohemian ambassador whirled around, one of his hands clearly resting on the hidden sheath at his side. "Who are you?"

Naděžda offered a gasp of surprise. "Why, this is my guard," she exclaimed, managing to smile graciously up at the ambassador, who was still concerned about the interruption.

"Are you sure, miss?"

"Of course I am sure," Naděžda replied soothingly. "What a happy coincidence this turned out to be, my dear Dolf—I mean, Mr. Svoboda."

Her flirtatious blush at calling him by his Christian name allowed the ambassador to be distracted again, long enough for Amir to take another step forward. He bowed to Naděžda, hiding his face from her as much as he was

17

avoiding her burning stare. He spoke to her in rapid Arabic, meaningless words of how her family will be upset at her disappearance and so worried—nothing that, should someone overhear them, would be anything near suspicious—before Naděžda laughed.

"I'm so sorry for the trouble." Naděžda did not look one bit sorry as she slipped her arm out of the ambassador's and into Amir's. "Thank you once more, Mr. Svoboda. I cannot thank you enough for seeing to my safety. It seems my family is waiting and I must go at once."

"I see." The ambassador frowned. "I see. Well, I am terribly sorry, Miss Cerná, that I did not get a chance to buy you the flowers I'd promised you."

"Oh, well, the book more than makes up for it," Naděžda insisted, holding up his gift. "I will have something to read while I pass the time in traveling back to London."

"You are headed for London?" he asked.

"Yes, and I will think of you the whole way there as I read through *The Prelude*," she gushed. "Perhaps before too long, I will be back in Prague, and I will be able to tell you all about it. That is, of course, so long as your wife approves."

"I regret to say so, but I do not have a wife."

For the first time, Naděžda looked truly surprised. Amir had to smother a laugh at her discomfort. He wondered if there was ever a time when she had received that particular response.

"Oh, my apologies, sir. I was certain a man of your status and knowledge must surely have a wife waiting eagerly for your return," she said, recovering nicely.

"No, I am afraid I have experienced several setbacks in my life, and I have been waiting for the right moment—and the right woman—to come along." The ambassador gave her a

18

hopeful new look. "Perhaps, if you do come to Prague, you will call upon me? And if not there, the Emperor has sent me all over Eastern Europe, and occasionally London as well."

"Well, if that is the case, I will be sure to look you up," Naděžda said.

"Thank you, my dear," Adolf said, taking her hand and bowing over it gallantly. "And when we do meet again, I will see to it that you have all the flowers a true lady like you deserves."

Amir looked at the poor, besotted smile on the ambassador's face. Amir had to remind himself not to give away the game, and punching the ambassador senseless would most certainly do just that.

THE ORDER OF THE CRYSTAL DAGGERS

3

◊

"Amir, let me go." After a few blocks of practically dragging her behind him, it was clear Naděžda's patience had reached its limit.

Amir's grip tightened at her irritation. "No."

She pulled back, but he did not let her go until they turned down another street.

"Amir, really, what was that about? You could have let me invite myself along to his meeting, and then I would have been able to sit down in the meeting itself."

"You don't need to go prostituting yourself out like that," Amir snapped. "That man was likely one step away from proposing, and the last thing a member of the Order such as yourself needs to worry about is marriage entanglements."

She seemed surprised, but it took her less than a moment to regroup and retaliate.

"Well done, Amir. I think you have my mother's impression near perfect," she countered, her own anger creeping into her voice. "Maybe you should put on her dress and rummage around in her rouge supply to get the full effect."

"Are you even listening to me?" Amir turned her around forcing her into a small garden, one that was hidden from the street by an intricate lattice fence. "You gave that man your name and let him walk you all throughout the town. Isn't that bad enough?"

"He was a perfectly fine gentleman," Naděžda hissed. "I'm not worried about my reputation anyway. Didn't you just hear yourself? What do I have to worry about, as a spy for the Order? I'm not going to get married."

He paused for a moment, realizing she was right, but he pressed on. After all the unpleasantness he had felt at her performance, he was not about to let her escape some sort of retribution. "It's my job to protect you."

"You needn't worry about doing such a thorough job on the matter." She jerked her hands free. "You could risk the mission."

"Mr. Prasad and Her Grace will be upset with me if anything happens to you."

She put her hands on her hips. "Well, then, I guess you do have plenty of reasons to be concerned about me after all. I know I wouldn't want to be on the receiving end of their hatred."

"No, you wouldn't." Amir glared at her. "Now, before we get too distracted by your boredom and penchant for leading men on, we have to circle around and find the Marmora pier and see if we can find that missing shipment of weapons that was supposed to be headed for Prague."

"Yes, yes, by all means, let's get to business," she huffed. "Forget prostituting myself out to a man, let's get on with prostituting myself out to the Order."

She pushed past him, letting *The Prelude* fall out of her hands and onto the ground as she passed him. Amir gazed at it for a long moment, before he swiftly kicked his foot out, pushing the book under another lattice. The book disappeared underneath a curtain of twisted vines, overgrown and burned by the summer's heat.

A sense of angry righteousness blistered through him. He had dismissed Naděžda's risky ventures and chastised her as a fool, and it was only fitting that she should suffer more. All

21

THE ORDER OF THE CRYSTAL DAGGERS

that time she had spent, and they could have just as easily followed the ambassador to the docks.

I don't need this. Amir watched as Naděžda stomped away from him.

His life had been perfectly fine before he had met Naděžda, he thought. He had grown up in a good home, not that far from the city streets of Constantinople.

He glanced down the streets; they were busier than ever, but he knew it would be easy to find his way back to his mother and father's house, if he wanted. He was even more certain his parents were at home, working diligently as ever as they attended to their duties.

He could see the picture in his mind as clearly as if it was before him. His beloved Ammi would be attending to the house, as she had done for all the years of his life, while his father would be at work, tending to patients and their medical needs. Amir could have easily gone home and joined his father. As Abba's only son and heir, Amir was expected to follow in his father's footsteps and become a doctor—a path he did not mind at all. When he had been younger, it was something he enjoyed. The first time he had feel completely happy and comfortable had been at his father's side, tending to the health of others, even the various foreigners who sought out his father's skill.

By the time his father started working under Harshad and Her Grace, Lady Penelope, unknowingly assisting the Order of the Crystal Daggers, the plan was that Amir would finish his education in the West, return home, and resume working with his father. Then he would marry and start his own family with a bride from a neighboring family.

But Amir knew he did not want to go home and see his family now.

Briefly, his eyes fell to the ground.

THE ORDER OF THE CRYSTAL DAGGERS

He loved his parents. He had always sought to do his duty to them. He did not want to upset them or disappoint them.

But all the answers to the riddles of his life became clear the instant he had laid eyes on Naděžda.

That was the moment the neat and orderly lines of his life—the boundaries between his home, work, and even his identity—suddenly faded in their sternness, overtaken by the bold stripe of irrepressible paint that Naděžda proved to be.

How did one go back to only a life of shadows after finding a rainbow, even if it was one he would never catch, but instead spend his life chasing?

She was as jarring as she was beautiful, an irresistible puzzle that left him frustrated and even more perplexed. She was rude and smart, flirtatious and vivacious and unapologetically insightful.

How could he explain to his parents how he'd felt in that moment?

And even now, he thought, when she was angry, she carried herself in a way that only made him want to apologize and beg her to smile and argue with him again.

No wonder she does not respect me. He grimaced, realizing he sounded like a fool, even to himself.

But if he was a fool, he was a fool for her. She was the answer to a question he never dared to ask, maybe even one he never wanted to ask, but one he did not dare ignore. And that made his shame a badge of honor, one he carried next to his heart.

He watched her, as she walked down through another bazaar. Her stride had slowed since she had pulled away from him.

He grinned; despite everything, she was waiting for him.

23

THE ORDER OF THE CRYSTAL DAGGERS

"Naděžda." Her name was a caress on the wind as he moved to catch up to her.

But before he could get far, a shadow suddenly reached out.

Darkness shifted, moving from an amorphous shape to a hand, one that wrapped around his wrist and yanked him out of the street.

Amir struggled to find his balance as his attacker slammed him into the wall of a wooden house.

"Ouch." Amir grunted as the lattice wall behind him cracked under his weight.

He quickly shrugged off his pain, moving into a fighting position. He'd been caught by surprise, but that did not mean he had none of his own.

The attacker in front of him was ready; he grabbed Amir's arm, turning and twisting it back. His enemy's hand drilled into his pressure point, making Amir grimace in silent pain.

He slid his feet out to the side, enough to make his attacker stumble.

Amir's eyes narrowed at his opponent's tiny wobble.

There it is ... an opening!

Amir lunged forward, forcing his enemy to move. He caught him off guard, long enough to force him into a new direction.

The attacker recovered, but not before Amir whirled around, slid his dagger free, and ducked low for his strike.

Amir prepared to feel the heavy impact of his dagger slicing through flesh, but his assailant was prepared for the offensive. He stepped to the side, pulled out a sword of his own, and grabbed him by the front of his shirt, and hurried to slice his throat.

24

THE ORDER OF THE CRYSTAL DAGGERS

Amir, completely surprised, leaned back as best as he could. It just registered inside his mind that he could die, as he felt the coolness of the sword's double-edged blade press into his neck.

There was just enough pressure to make him gulp nervously.

His attacked pulled away. "You are distracted today, Amir."

At the familiar voice, Amir almost chuckled with relief.

The sword dropped as the assailant stepped back. The mask fell away, and Amir watched as the beautiful sunstone eyes of Li Xiana glittered fiercely into his.

Seeing his old sparring partner, Amir grinned. "I should have guessed that was you, *saghira*. Even if you are set on fighting in those trousers."

She wrapped the fabric of her mask back around her neck before pulling down the turban she was wearing over her forehead, easily covering the last of her silken hair. While Amir could still make out the feminine features of her eyebrows and the delicate aloofness of her chin, Amir knew no one would think she was anything but another businessman walking through the streets. She wore the loose robes and long pants of a merchant, all at once both colorful and dark in their arrangement.

The mask was a nice touch, Amir had to admit, considering there were some men who took to covering their faces as the women did.

Xiana's face tilted forward, ever so slightly in a gracious nod, but her lips tightened into a slim line. "I do wish you would stop calling me your little sister, Amir. We have both grown since Harshad finished training us."

"It appears I may need a refresher, after your near success."

25

THE ORDER OF THE CRYSTAL DAGGERS

"I knew you would fail to notice me," Xiana said, glancing back toward the street, where Naděžda was. "You always had a weakness for skirts on a lady."

Her tone was never more inflicted than she wanted it, and Amir did not know if she was laughing at him or if she was accusing him.

"Is that why you decided to say hello as roughly as you did? To test me?" He rubbed his shoulder, massaging the place where Xiana had drilled her pernicious fingers into his joint only a moment before.

He caught sight of her *jian* again as she sheathed it. "Or was it perhaps to test your own skills with a new sword?"

"I will not do it next time," she assured him, ignoring his comment. "You were distracted, but I can see you've managed to keep most of Harshad's lessons at the forefront of your mind with fighting, even though they did not serve you as well as they should have."

"Perhaps it is Her Grace's lessons on espionage I need to keep better," Amir conceded.

Xiana frowned. "It would be easier for you, if you did not let her daughter upset you so."

Amir coughed, trying to fight off the urge to blush. "Miss Eleanor is not accustomed to the clime of the city, I am afraid. When she is upset, it is very often that everyone else is, too."

"You are better than that."

"Most days, perhaps. But not all."

The two of them stepped out around the corner, watching as Naděžda continued to bustle through the marketplace, with several vendors between them. As Amir watched, she stopped to look over an array of fruit, inspecting them carefully.

"She has noticed you are not following her," Xiana said. "I should let you get back to your mission."

"You won't be joining us?"

Xiana shook her head. "Not for the moment," she said. She pulled a small pouch out from behind her and held it up. "While he is with Lady Penelope, meeting with some of the Chinese dockmasters, Harshad wanted me to get more herbs. The silver thallis supply Lady Penelope keeps is in need of replenishing."

"I thought she had a delivery of it back in her townhouse in London a few months ago. Why does she need more?"

"The silver thallis needs to be fresh when it is used," Xiana said. "If you wait too long, it loses its potency. It poisons the bloodstream but does not cause death. The body is able to remove it after a few weeks and eventually, the intended victim is able to heal."

"I see. I didn't know that."

"Many women have used it in disposing of their lovers' babes," Xiana said. Amir winced at her tone; it was entirely too straightforward, especially when considering the topic. "It seems there are many things you still have to learn about herbs and their properties."

"The silver thallis is a rare herb, and one without any healing properties. It really isn't that unusual I'd never learned about it before working with the Order."

Xiana arched a brow. "Some women would say it heals them of the shame of an unwanted pregnancy."

"But pregnancy is still a natural process, not an illness in itself." Amir held up his hands. "If the herb could cure battle wounds and venereal diseases, it would be more common knowledge among doctors such as myself."

27

"Once we are finished here, perhaps I will be able to teach you more."

"Are you joining us in heading back to London after we find out where the missing shipment went?" Amir asked. "I know Her Grace is eager to get back home."

"Perhaps I will come, especially if you will be going." Xiana's eyes slid over to meet his accusingly. "Why are you going back to London? What of your family here?"

She knew him too well, Amir thought with a smile. "I know it seems strange to you, but I do not like having a family all the time."

"That would be strange to me, considering I do not have a family as you do," Xiana easily agreed. "But that does not mean I am unable to understand the burdens of duty. Lady Penelope and Harshad have become my family, and I strive to do all I can to please them."

"Even if it means forgoing your own happiness?" Amir asked.

"Especially then," she said, her voice dark and almost bitter.

"Well, then, you know exactly what I feel." Amir patted her shoulder companionably. "I will see you back at the ship, *saghira*."

"Amir." Her voice went flat. "Do not think of me as your sister. We might both share a debt to Lady Penelope and Harshad, but the last thing in this world we are is brother and sister."

Amir was struck by her harsher tone, and immediately bowed his head in apology. "If that is your wish. I beg your pardon."

"You have it," Xiana murmured. "But that is not my only wish, and I wish you would see that, as well."

28

THE ORDER OF THE CRYSTAL DAGGERS

"Wishes are oddly burdensome things." Amir glanced down the street at Naděžda, watching her pay for an apple at a vendor. She had used another one of his coins, he noticed.

But as she lowered her mask and took a bite out of the apple, her eyes met his in the most daring of challenges, and Amir felt it was well worth the price.

"I can see you are anxious to get back to your charge," Xiana said, her voice as stoic as ever. "Excuse me."

"Farewell," Amir replied. As Xiana pushed past him, he flinched at the sudden, sharp pain his arm. He had not been expecting her departure to be painful.

Of course, I was not expecting her arrival to be, either. He rubbed the back of his shoulder where her earlier attack did the most of its damage before checking over his throat, just to make sure her blade did not actually cut him.

He watched Xiana as she walked down the street, her gait quick and rigid—nothing like the other men surrounding them.

She was not usually so careless, Amir thought. He wondered if he was not the only one who was distracted.

He shrugged it off a moment later. There were always any number of complications that came with missions, and for all her skill and undeniable prowess, Xiana had been known to end up fighting for her results more often than not.

Amir turned back toward the market, eager to give his attention back to Naděžda.

Only to find she was nowhere in sight.

4

◊

Amir felt pure, raging panic as it flared up inside him. His vision sharpened, his eyes scourging the different vendors for a sign of Naděžda and her striped gown. As he raked his gaze over the scene before him, his nerves blistered, both in anger and fear—anger at the thought she would taunt him this way, leaving him behind as a punishment for his own neglect and their earlier disagreements, and fear that in losing sight of her, she might truly be in danger.

Where is she? Where did she go?

Amir tightened his grip on his dagger as he hurried toward the fruit vendor, weaving through the different clusters of shoppers and citizens. He had several people glance in his way, and he struggled to keep his expression calm and focused. But the more carefully he looked around, the more worried he became.

A small flicker of red caught his eye from the side of the street as he approached the corner.

Amir swallowed hard as he walked over and knelt down. It was the apple he'd seen her purchase, rolling idly on the side of the street, the missing bite she'd taken glaringly white against its distinctive redness. He picked it up, running his fingertips over it carefully, allowing himself to linger over the place where her lips had touched it.

Where could she be? Why wasn't I there to protect her?

He stood up, whirling around, desperate to find her.

"Naděžda!" The gnawing sickness in his gut grew exponentially, as she was nowhere to be found. Fear choked him as his anger was instantly forgotten.

A voice spoke up from behind him.

"Are you searching for the Western woman?"

Amir turned to see an older, dark-skinned woman on the ground, not far from the corner. He paused momentarily, recalling the inferior reputation of those who were slaves, or former slaves as this woman appeared to be. As he took in her whole appearance, he realized that there was another reason to hesitate; she was a fortune teller, and those who dabbled with devils were not to be trusted.

As if sensing his concern, the old lady laughed dryly. "Not afraid of an old negress like me more than you are of losing your lady, are you?"

Amir carefully studied the woman. He still did not trust her, but she was right about Naděžda. He had to find her, and if that meant getting help from disreputable sources, so be it.

"No," he said, stepping forward. "Please, I need your help."

"Given the fight your lady put up, I would agree," she said. "A pure-hearted man such as you is no doubt worried about recovering what is his."

Amir blushed. "She is not—"

The fortune teller arched her thin, white brows at him as she played with the cards in her hands. "Isn't she though?"

Amir said nothing to that. It was too complicated to explain to the woman, and he feared he did not have the time to indulge her.

"Please," he said. "Please tell me what you saw."

"There were some men who approached your lady. She resisted them, but when they surrounded her, she drew them into a corner."

Amir felt his hands tingle with fear and rage. "What happened?"

31

THE ORDER OF THE CRYSTAL DAGGERS

"Your lady is quite a fighter." The old fortune teller pointed down toward the Bosporus. "After they subdued her, they hauled her into a wagon and headed that way. I could hear the one say they were going to the docks where the other traders were."

"Do you know which ship they were on?"

She shook her head. "They are as cunning as they are varied, but they likely took your lady to the far end of the port, where the other slave traders are."

"Slave traders?" Amir felt the blood drain from his face.

"You are not from here, are you? The trade of women and children is very profitable here." The older woman's face grew more careworn as Amir's heart constricted.

The fortune teller rubbed her gnarled hands together, before laying out her pinkish palms before her apologetically. "Too many years in the British Empire, perhaps? They might have outlawed slavers, but the rest of the world continues the practice. Those in power will always want dominion those weaker than they are, and that includes the men who sell women."

Amir was shamed to realize how much of his own culture he had forgotten over the years.

He bowed low to the woman. "Thank you for your help," he said. "I will find a way to repay you, I promise."

The woman smiled at him, clearly delighted by his respectful manners. "You do not need to worry about it, young man. It's not as though you asked me for your fortune."

"There is no price I wouldn't pay to keep my lady safe," Amir whispered.

"Then it hardly seems fair for me to give you one, is there?" The lady's expression, hardened by years of working and

32

disillusionment, warmed as she looked at him. "*Allah yusallmak.* If what you say is true, I suspect you know the trouble you will find as you keep your word."

"Thank you." Amir gave her one more bow and hurried off toward the docks, desperate to find Naděžda.

◊   ◊   ◊   ◊

If Amir suspected time had slowed before out of spite, he was certain it began to speed up with a vengeance as he hurried down to the far point of the Marmora Pier. He was out of breath as he arrived, just in time to hear the *Maghrib* call to prayer ring out around him.

He stopped at the street up from the docks, looking over the area with unappreciative scrutiny. The welcoming background of the Ottoman Empire greeted the newcomers as they stepped off their ships, while the subtle dirt of the city clung to the streets. Ships of all sizes were both pulling into safe harbor and heading out to sea as merchants and more scrambled around. Several called out their sales pitches as the crowds passed by.

It could have been any ordinary afternoon, Amir thought with a grimace.

How am I supposed to find Naděžda in all of this?

He stood there, stymied, out of breath and nearly out of hope. Amir tightened his grip on his dagger, running his hands over the inscriptions once more, searching for any sign of divine assistance. There were no prayers he knew to recite that asked for such a request to be granted.

Amir closed his eyes, picturing Naděžda. Her own eyes looked back at him, full of a vulnerability he wanted to believe he was only imagining. She was only twenty, he remembered, thinking of her youthful innocence, but he

33

almost always forgot she was two years younger. With her spirit and stubbornness, she always seemed so much older than she was.

And much more capable, too, Amir thought bitterly. He should have known better than to let her out of his sight, even for a moment.

"Please," he prayed quietly. "Please help me find her."

An eerie silence seemed to settle around him, as the activity of the docks fell into whispers.

Was that his answer?

Amir opened his eyes, defeated, feeling more helpless and alone than ever. He slumped over, wondering if this was his punishment for loving Naděžda. It was too easy to think so. Too much of their lives would keep them apart, and it could only end badly.

"*Stop!*"

Amir's head snapped up, as he straightened. Naděžda's voice, strong and sharp, cut through the silence around him. All distractions were pushed to the side as he heard her voice.

She was nowhere in sight, but he hurried off, heading in the direction where he heard her voice. There was nothing in front of him as he stepped out in faith.

He clenched his fists as he ran, more determined than ever. There was so much that kept them apart, Amir thought. But if there was anything that could bridge the chasm between them, it was surely love.

And he loved her. Irrevocably, undeniably, he loved her, and he would find her, if only to tell her how much he needed her in his life.

Amir slowed his pace as he came up beside another teak-hulled ship designed for warmer waters. He was certain he

THE ORDER OF THE CRYSTAL DAGGERS

was lost. There was no sign of Naděžda; it became increasingly obvious he had imagined her voice, driven out of his desperation.

He was about to head down the docks when he glanced saw a pair of stocks.

Slave traders.

Amir stared at the empty stocks, suddenly sickened. This was the place where they would auction off their prisoners. There was no one around—there was no sign at all that any such an event had taken place in recent hours—but as he made his way toward the stocks, he saw a man pass by.

Amir did not recognize him, but with his tunic and military-style jacket, the man wore clothes similar to the Bohemian ambassador. He seemed out of place, as if he was looking for something, too.

Instantly, a thousand different possibilities came rushing through Amir's mind, and he did not know which was worse.

Was it possible Adolf Svoboda was too enchanted with the lady with the fallen flowers? Could he have sent his guards to go and kidnap her, under the disguise slave traders?

"I knew she shouldn't have talked with him," he murmured. "I'll strangle her for this when I get her back."

Amir trailed after the man, following at a safe distance as the man came up to a warehouse. Amir watched as the man walked inside, and Amir took a deep breath.

He could follow the man, but the more that time passed, the more nervous he felt. Amir did not want to lose Naděžda. What if this was just wasting his time?

He sighed. There was nothing else to do, he thought. He would have to search the docks, one ship at a time. There was no reason he could not start where he was.

35

THE ORDER OF THE CRYSTAL DAGGERS

With that renewed determination, Amir made his way to the back of the warehouse.

The instant he opened the door, and the chilly shadows of the building enveloped him, chains rattled. There *was* someone there! Amir silently cheered as he squinted into the darkness.

"Naděžda?" he whispered.

The voice that greeted him squashed his fledgling hope.

"Finally!" A man huffed indignantly. "I have been waiting for someone to let me go. I can assure you, sir, your masters have made a grave mistake, and I am ecstatic to see there is someone intelligent enough among you to correct such a sinful grievance."

Amir frowned, but before he could say anything else, the man continued talking.

"Now, if you would be so good as to hurry, my good sir, and release me from these chains, I am in desperate need of refreshment. This is a silk shirt, and I can assure you, this place was not made to accommodate me at all. I need to get back to my ship."

"Which ship is yours?" Amir asked. He took a cautious step closer.

"The steamer, of course," the man replied. "I only buy the best and newest models for myself."

"If you are so rich, why are you in here?" Amir took another step closer, finally able to see the man's face.

He could see the piercing green eyes of a gentlemen, one who was educated in the best and possibly worse sort of ways; there was no room for innocence in the prisoner's gaze. He was indeed, wearing a silk shirt, and he looked as though he had been dragged out of a harem; his shirt was only buttoned halfway up his chest, and his breeches, cut in the

36

French style, were on backwards. As Amir watched him, the man flipped a long flop of his hair upward in exasperation.

"I suppose you're after some kind of reward?" The man rolled his eyes. "Well, I suppose I can't blame you there, but really, I have to say I'm disappointed you're not going to do the right thing without financial incentive."

"I am looking for someone else," Amir said, unsure of why he was talking to this prisoner at all.

"I see. Well then, you've found the right person indeed," the man replied. "I am Lumiere Valoris, and I am more or less in charge of everything down here by the Marmora."

"How are you in charge of everything?" Amir asked. "You're not the sultan."

"Abdülmecid is terribly busy, trying to turn his Empire into Europe without anyone noticing," Lumiere scoffed. "He is like any other ruler—content to believe himself to be in charge of everything, even if he is not. I am the richest man here, thanks to my family's holdings across Europe. Tell me what you need, and I will give it to you."

"I am looking for a woman," Amir said. "She was taken, possibly by slave traders."

"Psh. There are no slave traders here while the East India Company is in port," Lumiere said. "My father's one of the people who negotiated that deal, thanks to his connections to the French and British Empires."

"France is no longer an empire."

"So you think," Lumiere said with another smirk. "Just you wait. Napoleon's legacy is not finished yet."

"I'll have to worry about that later," Amir said. He stepped back, heading toward the door, wondering if he would be able to find the Bohemian man again. "Right now, I need to find my friend. She is my business partner. I wish you well, sir."

"No, wait." Lumiere's voice was suddenly more desperate as Amir turned to leave. "They'll kill me if you leave me here."

"Why?"

"There are certain laws you can't break while you're here, and let's just say, I'm not excited about the thought of a public execution, no matter how *smashing* it might be." Lumiere's wide eyes, framed with kohl and aided by the rogue on his cheeks, seemed younger than before as he looked at Amir. "If you get me out of here, I'll help you find your partner. I promise. I will use my connections to help you."

Amir hesitated. Once more, he was faced with the thought of getting aid from someone he did not trust, and this time, it was a villain of sorts.

But as he studied Lumiere's face—seeing the pleading smolder, his roughened form, and his swaggering entitlement—Amir reluctantly softened.

He gave in, quickly using his dagger to pick through the chains, cutting them off at the manacles.

"Can't you remove these beastly things?" Lumiere complained.

"Can't you just find a way to pay someone else to do it later?" Amir asked. "Right now, you need to help me."

"I see you've failed to appreciate just how much I have suffered in the last two days," Lumiere balked. "I must get back to my father's ship if I am to return to Bohemia."

"Bohemia?" Amir quickly shook his head and dismissed the information. He did not have time to wonder about his mission now, not when Naděžda still had to be found. "What about your promise?"

Lumiere waved his arm aside, his rogued lips tightening with displeasure. "The word of a Frenchman is one thing, but his timing is another, my good sir, and you must excuse me in this manner."

"No." Amir took out his dagger, brandishing it in front of Lumiere. "This is too important."

Lumiere stared down at him for a long moment, before he growled. "Fine. Let's go. But I warn you, I must hurry. I've got a shipment of stolen weapons heading out of port, and I don't need my father haranguing me for the delay."

"Wait." Amir grabbed Lumiere's shirt, holding his dagger up to his chest. "You have a shipment of stolen weapons?"

"Oh, goodness. Don't tell me one of the sultan's few competent policemen is my rescuer today." Lumiere grabbed Amir's wrist and stepped back, easily untangling himself. "How do you think my family got rich?"

Amir gritted his teeth together. "We can discuss it later," he snapped. "Right now, I need your help. If you're as rich and powerful as you say, you will stop all port activity until my partner is returned to me."

"We'll see about that," Lumiere murmured. "But if you want my help now, you'll have to drop your charges against me later."

"Only if you deliver," Amir warned. "Or I will make sure you suffer."

"Hey, I am *already* suffering, and of complete boredom, no less," Lumiere whined. "Let's just go. At least escaping here and looking for your partner will be more exciting that standing here and arguing with the likes of you."

39

THE ORDER OF THE CRYSTAL DAGGERS

5

◊

Amir did not have to question how desperate he was as he raced along the port with Lumiere behind him. As they left the building—loudly, to the objection of several of the men inside who were supposed to be guarding him—Amir was beginning to wonder if he had done the right thing in letting Lumiere go.

"Wouldn't happen to have a pistol on you, would you?" Lumiere asked, as they ran from a pair of Bohemian guards. "I'm a crack shot, and it would be easier to get rid of the king's supporters."

"No," Amir called back. "If you're going to Bohemia, why are those guards chasing you?"

"Didn't you hear me? Those are Bohemian loyalists. They came with the king's ambassador, and they think they're doing the sultan a favor by catching deviants like myself and trading me off to the local authorities. Never mind that I control half the Ottoman's profits in Constantinople."

"Those are the Bohemian ambassador's guards." Amir was grateful for the confirmation, even though he did not know what to think about it. He decided he would ask Harshad later, after he found Naděžda.

"Yes, and they're quite upset, too. Probably needed someone like me to tamper the crushing blow they're going to deliver to King Ferdinand."

"Crushing blow?"

"Let's just say not everyone in Bohemia wants a revolution, but those who are not prepared for it are going to get hit the hardest." Lumiere snorted disdainfully. "They call him

40

'Ferdinand the Good,' but personally, I prefer the name 'Ferdinand the Good-for-Nothing.'"

Amir said nothing; he knew there was plenty of unrest in Bohemia, same as several other nations. While there was likely to be enough blame on both sides, he had a feeling there would be no easy answer.

"Say, my good sir, what is your name, anyway?" Lumiere asked. "I'm getting tired of pretending I respect you."

Amir sniffed. "I saved your life."

"There are plenty who would say my life is of no consequence."

"My name is Amir." As they ducked around another building, Amir held out his hand in greeting. Lumiere shook it as they stopped.

"Good to know." Lumiere straightened as he glanced around. "I need to get back to the *Chaos*. It's nearly dark, and I need to get into my formal clothes."

"Formal clothes?"

"What am I? A commoner?" Lumiere shook his head. "I might have to work, but it's at my pleasure that I do so."

"I assume that your pleasure is the reason you were caught, too?" Amir asked.

"Don't you know me so well already?"

Amir flinched at the thought. "You can go back to your ship once I find my partner."

"Good," Lumiere said. "I'm starting to get annoyed by you. But then, men of honor are frequently annoying. And I suppose looking for a woman would do that to you."

"This is not just any woman," Amir said. "She is too important to me."

THE ORDER OF THE CRYSTAL DAGGERS

"Yes, yes, I know." Lumiere rolled his eyes. "Women. Who needs them, anyway?"

Amir frowned at him, but Lumiere grabbed his arm and tugged him down another street.

"Come, Amir," Lumiere said. "I will show you where all the contraband tends to run. If what you say is true, and she was taken by the slave traders, that is where she will be."

"I thought you said your father made it so there were no slaves at port while the British and French were around?"

"Sovereignty of nations is always a tricky thing," Lumiere said with a shrug. "Sovereignty of individuals? Even worse. Thank the good Lord for human stupidity, or I would feel the world itself would be in danger."

"As opposed to only human life?"

Lumiere grinned at Amir's irritated tone. "Of course."

Amir did his best to ignore Lumiere as they made their way through the different piers. He kept a sharp eye out for Naděžda, hoping against hope it seemed, that he would find her without needing any assistance from Lumiere. He did not want to pray for more help; he was worried that in letting Lumiere go, he had already invited the devil along with him.

"Tell me about this woman," Lumiere said, pulling Amir out of his thoughts.

"She's the daughter of a duchess." He did not want Lumiere to think this was anything he could take flippantly.

"She's the daughter of a duchess, but works with you as a partner?" Lumiere frowned. "That must mean she's actually adopted, or possibly born on the wrong side of the blanket."

Lumiere's green eyes twinkled in suspicion. "Why are you really here? What is your partner's name?"

THE ORDER OF THE CRYSTAL DAGGERS

"Her name is Eleanor Ollerton-Cerná," Amir said, struggling to keep his voice professional. "She is working with me on—"

"Ollerton? As in Ollerton-Wellesley?" Lumiere stopped short. He suddenly bent over, guffawing with laughter. "Oh, Lord, this is too precious!"

Amir stiffened. "What's so funny?"

"You." Lumiere gripped onto his stomach as he laughed uproariously. "I told you, I am the one who knows everything that goes on in this port. If you're looking for the offspring of an Ollerton and a Cerná, I'm more than willing to bet my men picked her up."

"What are you talking about?"

"I'm Lumiere *Valoris*," he said, emphasizing his last name. When Amir only gave him a blank look, he laughed harder. "You are Lady Penelope's stooge, and you've never heard of me?"

Amir frowned.

"Oh my goodness, this is so amusing." Lumiere wiped the tears from his eyes. "Well, I can't help you any further than this, I'm afraid."

"What?" Amir grabbed his arm, pushing him into the ground. "You promised me."

"I'm shocked a man working with the Order of the Crystal Daggers is so obtuse," Lumiere snapped, his tone suddenly much harder as Amir pushed him onto his knees. "Hey, watch the clothes. It would take a nice chunk out of the Iron Dowager's coffers to replace them."

Amir ignored him and, instead, tightened his grip. "How do you know about Her Grace?"

THE ORDER OF THE CRYSTAL DAGGERS

Lumiere shook his head. "Those who don't know their history are destined to make their future worse."

"What is that supposed to mean?" Amir's impatience was creeping in. "Never mind. I've had enough. Tell me where my partner is, or I will end your life here and now."

"Hardly. You're not going to do it out in public like this," Lumiere argued. He broke Amir's hold and stood up, brushing himself off indignantly. "Come. I'll take you to my father's traders. They're the ones who likely have her. They were warned the Order would try to interfere with their goals if they weren't careful."

"What are you talking about?" Amir frowned, following as Lumiere pushed himself through the crowds.

"I'm talking about a chess game," Lumiere said. "One that does not play with little pieces on a board, but one that is silently being played out between several parties, over the nation of Europe and its trading partners all around the world. I know your leader, Lady Penelope, would like to believe she's got the upper hand now that she's secured herself in working with the Order and the League, but there are plenty in the League who do not like her—perhaps especially including her former lover, Jakub Cerný, and my father, Louis Valoris."

Amir recognized the name of Naděžda's father, but the other name was foreign to him. "The League? You mean the League of Ungentlemanly Warfare?"

"Of course. She might be scheming her way in, but she will always be an outsider. Not even her former lover, Jakub Cerný, will be able to help her. In fact, he's likely a detriment now."

"Are you working with the League, too, then?"

"Ha! I am working for myself, at my pleasure, remember?" Lumiere glanced over his shoulder long enough to give Amir a sneer. "The League should be so lucky, shouldn't it?"

"You know of Her Grace, Lady Penelope."

"Yes, I do, and I would normally question anyone who works with her. In fact, why would a Turk such as yourself be content to work for a woman, and a British one at that? Especially as a babysitter for her daughter, like you've hinted?"

"I have my own reasons, just as you have your own reasons for finding pleasure in ruining others' lives," Amir retorted.

"There's no need to sound judgmental," Lumiere replied. "Suffering is supposed to be a great teacher. I am only helping the populace. They will appreciate their prosperity much more later on, thanks to my efforts."

"Ha!" Amir shook his head.

"Oh, stop," Lumiere said. "Look, I'm helping you, aren't I? And against my father's wishes, too. You should be thanking me profusely, even swearing your allegiance to me, for all I'm doing for you."

"I'm the one who saved *you*, if you'll recall."

"That happened, what? Ten minutes ago?"

"It could be an eternity at this point," Amir grumbled.

"Exactly," Lumiere said. "No need to worry about it now, do we? Especially when we have someone else to save."

"Just get us there, and then I will release you from the rest of your promise," Amir said.

"If those are your terms, I formally accept." Lumiere grinned. "Once I have my freedom, I do believe my friendship will be a much more valuable asset."

45

Amir did not want to believe Lumiere was serious. He was grateful that the rest of their trip was made mostly in silence, though Lumiere tried to engage Amir by making random comments from time to time. As they approached his ship, the *Chaos*, Amir coughed at the coal pouring into the air from the funnels. The smoky lines rising up from the ship clouded the skies, almost giving the impression it was nighttime.

"Keep your voice down," Lumiere said, waving his arm dismissively as they came up to a loading house.

Amir shot Lumiere an angry glare, but he said nothing else.

"Come this way." Lumiere led Amir back behind the building. He motioned to Amir to keep silent, as they hurried to the back door.

This time, the door was locked.

As Lumiere struggled to open the door in a clumsy manner, Amir groaned. He wondered if he had done the right thing again. How could he really trust Lumiere? There was nothing about him that Amir even wanted to trust him with, and yet, here he was, practically following him to the ends of the earth.

Which, Amir reminded himself, was exactly how far he would go to protect Naděžda.

What if she had escaped the men who had caught her? What if she was back with Harshad and Lady Penelope now, resting on their own ship as he searched the city for her?

The dread in his heart contradicted that vision, even if he hoped with all his soul it was true.

"Got it," Lumiere cheered, as the door opened up. He stepped back and pointed inside. "This is where we take care of the more unpleasant sides of business. If we have her, she'll be in there. Lady Penelope will be able to help you if she's not. If I ask anything of you, it is that you do not tell her you ran into me. If you want your deal to be fulfilled, actually, you will not say anything to her. She will be upset with me, as will my father, who will no doubt hear of this incident."

"Where are you going?" Amir asked, surprised to see Lumiere back away.

"I've got to get to the ship and change my clothes," he said.

"What?" Amir looked at him, incredulously. "That doesn't matter."

"Come now, I've explained this to you. These are my men, but they are paid by my father. I can't help you—not without risking my own neck and future in the process. I have paid my debt to you, and that is all I can do. If I am going to play the game here, this game of four-way or more-than-four-way chess, then I can't afford to lose, especially for something as silly as honor."

"But—"

"But nothing, Amir, my friend." Lumiere gave him a shrewd, appraising look. "It's been absolutely lovely to have a strong and loyal man such as you by my side. I hope we meet again, someday, when it will be better for us to be on the same side."

He reached out his hand, and Amir shook it politely, still dumbfounded that Lumiere was leaving him.

"Call me Lumi," Lumiere told him. "So I will know we are friends."

At the thought of being Lumiere's friend, Amir felt rather repulsed. But he nodded, despite his hesitation.

Lumiere smirked, letting his blond bangs flop forward, before his hand ran through his hair and pushed them back.

"Now, go and get your lady," Lumiere said. "I'm sure she'll be anxious to be saved. My father would be all too happy to

THE ORDER OF THE CRYSTAL DAGGERS

have her in his grasp, considering how much he hates her mother. And how much he'd love to send revolutions running through Europe, too."

Before Amir could say anything else, Lumiere slipped away, strutting with pride, heading back toward his ship.

Amir did not know how to process everything. He decided a moment later to worry about it after he had Naděžda back—if, indeed, Lumiere was right about where she was.

As if on a cue, a bloodcurdling scream rang out in pain, yelling from inside the loading station.

He recognized her voice at once, much as he had recognized her the day he'd first met her.

"Naděžda." Amir breathed in deeply, both in fear and in relief. He pulled out his dagger, letting the tip of the *Wahabite Jambiya* glimmer with the fading light of day before he entered the building.

6

◊

Amir raced through the halls, the gloomy, unfamiliar atmosphere pressing into him as he moved. The aura of grim and dirty business persisted through every inch of space around him, and he hated to think what sort of activities went on there on a regular basis.

He shook off his discomfort as much as he could, forcing himself to concentrate only on finding and rescuing Naděžda.

"You, there!" A voice called out just as Amir reached the end of the hallway. He stopped in front of a door, turning around just in time to see a pair of guards as they rushed after him. "Stop!"

He was able to briefly make out the French *fleur-de-lis* on the sleeves of their overcoats before they accosted him.

Amir allowed himself to be pushed against the doors, using their momentum and flurry to gain the upper hand. He caught them off guard, and as they stumbled forward, he ducked down and slashed his dagger across the back of their knees.

The men howled in pain, both of them falling away to the side. Amir said a silent prayer for their recovery, hating how sinful men sought to deter him from doing right. He pushed them away before he thrust open the doors.

Stepping into the next room, Amir scrambled to block the door; there was no lock, and the men who attacked him were calling for help on the other side. Once he knew he had bought himself enough time, Amir saw he'd come right into the heart of the loading dock.

All around him, large wooden crates marked over in a variety of languages were stacked high. He paused, waiting in the shadows of a tall tower of boxes, watching as a pair of men hauled another crate out of the large room. Some of the labels he recognized as part of the missing weapons shipment that was supposed to head to Bohemia.

Amir ran a hand over his chin ruefully. *Lumiere had been telling the truth.*

He was relieved, but he was also surprised; the incendiary Frenchman did not seem to be the type to tell the truth, unless it suited him.

Amir sighed. He would get a headache trying to figure out someone like Lumiere. He made a mental note to have Harshad send Xiana or some of their other associates over later. He gripped his dagger again, returning his focus to finding Naděžda.

As if to remind him, he heard Naděžda cry out from across the storage room.

"Stop!" Her voice was low, her teeth gritted in pain.

Amir nearly choked at the sound. He hurriedly swallowed his fear and made his way to the far end of the room, careful not to alert anyone else to his presence.

He came to the end a row of boxes, and he was suddenly able to see her.

"Naděžda."

He nearly turned away as he saw her. The sickness in his gut felt even worse.

Her hands were bound in a pair of stocks, as she knelt on the stand. The formal, striped outer layers of her gown had been stripped away along with her mask and headdress, leaving her in her petticoat and corset. The white of her pantalettes had speckles of blood that trickled down onto her garments from her back, where she had been whipped.

THE ORDER OF THE CRYSTAL DAGGERS

Amir felt the rage inside of him boil as a man stepped forward, carrying the whip in question. He wore a turban over his dark, scraggly hair, and his beard seemed to overgrow his face.

"Insolent woman!" The man cried out. "You dare mock me?"

Amir watched as Naděžda—his Naděžda, so proud and stubborn—lifted her chin defiantly to him.

"How can I resist?" she shouted back. "You have all the self-control of an infant, and the temper to go along with it. It's shameful that you should be bothered so much by a mere woman."

"You are no 'mere woman,'" the man replied, and Amir had to agree with him. "You managed to kill one of my men."

"Your man died because he couldn't swim," Naděžda shot back. "Not because I stopped him from apprehending me."

"You pushed him out of the wagon."

"It seemed prudent, considering he was the one who threw me into it against my wishes."

"What are a woman's wishes?" The foreman scoffed. "We might respect your privacy when you Western women play by our rules here, but we are still your masters."

He raised the whip to her again, and Amir couldn't watch as he brought it down on her. At her cry, Amir winced. He stepped back in horror, only to knock against a tall pile of crates.

The boxes shifted his impact, enough where they shook. Amir sized them up, while he heard Naděžda spit angrily at her opponent.

"You'll be sorry for that later," she said.

51

THE ORDER OF THE CRYSTAL DAGGERS

Amir prayed she would be right as he pushed on the stack of crates behind him. He felt a groan rise in his throat as he struggled to push them over.

"If you are going to try my patience, perhaps it is better I take care of breaking you before I turn you over to my captain."

Amir heard the slap of skin against tender flesh and pushed harder on the crates.

"You'll never break me," Naděžda said, her voice restrained, but lined with pain.

"We'll see about that."

Amir's eyes widened as he heard the sound of ripping fabric, and he knew Naděžda needed his help at once.

"Please," he murmured, slamming into the crates one last time.

They tumbled over, falling down and smashing open. Amir ducked behind another row as the foreman yelled and cursed, calling for his assistants. As their footsteps came closer, Amir sniffed, nearly sneezing at the dust and debris that littered the area in front of him. Careful to stay out of sight, he peeked around to see Naděžda was safe. The last of her crin petticoat had been torn away, fully exposing her pantalettes.

As the men and the foreman came closer to inspect him, Amir slipped out from his hiding place. Once he was sure they were sufficiently distracted, he quietly made his way to Naděžda.

She was breathing deeply, trying to remain calm, as he came up beside her.

Her head snapped up at his approach. "Stay away—"

Naděžda's words died on her lips as she saw him. There was nothing holding back the relief in her gaze. "Amir."

THE ORDER OF THE CRYSTAL DAGGERS

He nodded and put his finger to his lips, signaling her to be quiet as he used his dagger to dismantle the stocks.

"I was hoping you would come for me," she breathed. There was a dim sparkle in her eyes, and Amir was almost sickened by her doubt.

"You didn't think I would let anything happen to you, did you?" he asked.

"It was my fault for getting captured," Naděžda murmured. "You would have thought I deserved it."

Before Amir could shame her for such a thought, a shadow bore down on them.

"Watch out!" Naděžda pushed Amir away, allowing the whip to come down on her shoulder. As he rolled to his feet, Amir saw the whip lash around, cutting into her skin.

"Naděžda," he sputtered, horrified to see her bleed even more.

"So, the woman has a partner." The foreman stepped forward, holding his whip in one hand as he used his other hand to pull out a pistol. He cocked the gun and aimed it for Amir, as Naděžda screamed.

"No!" she cried, her one arm still stuck in the stock.

The foreman was distracted enough that Amir lunged at him.

The gun went off, crackling like lightning as the bullet ripped through the room. Amir felt the heat of the gun like it was a small explosion.

In that moment, he felt as though everything were happening all at once. The foreman's men behind him were rushing toward him, their own daggers high; Naděžda was still trapped, and the foreman was preparing to strike out with the whip once more.

THE ORDER OF THE CRYSTAL DAGGERS

Amir lunged forward, thrusting his dagger into the man's chest as he grabbed the hand that held the whip. Using his momentum, he whirled around, letting the whip strike his other adversaries.

The foreman's eyes went blank with death, and Amir shoved him away, pulling his blood-covered blade out of his enemy's chest. The other men backed up, faltering in their advance at the sign of their dead leader.

Amir was ready for them. He parried his dagger against the one man, while landing a kick squarely in the other man's torso, sending him falling backwards. His other opponent stepped forward, but Amir used his dagger to slice through his tunic.

The man looked at the stream of blood that spurted forward, and immediately stepped back.

"Go," Amir told him. "I am not here for you."

At his words, the two men exchanged a quick look, and then ran away.

Amir waited until they were out of the room and the door was shut behind them before he dropped his guarded stance and hurried back over to Naděžda.

She was staring at him, dumbfounded, as he severed through the last lock that held her captive. The moment she was free, she threw herself into his arms.

"Amir."

"I'm here." He tightened his arms around her and held onto her for a long moment as she fell against him. He allowed him that small moment of a reward, letting his face bury into the loosen tresses of her hair. Now that they were safe, all he wanted to do was hold her. He wanted nothing more than to run his hands all down her body and assure

THE ORDER OF THE CRYSTAL DAGGERS

himself she was real and she was alive, soothing over every inch of pain with his comfort and care.

He pulled back from her more than reluctantly. He pulled off his own tunic, letting himself embrace the small warmth of the saltwater breeze through the white shirt on underneath. Once he was sure she could stand, he pulled the jacket over her.

"Let's get back to the ship," he said, his voice hoarse as he picked her up and cradled her in his arms.

"Amir, wait." She glanced around. "This is the missing shipment of weapons. We need to find out who is behind this."

Amir tightened his grip on her as he walked past the boxes he had overturned. There was a keg of gunpowder near his foot, and he was more than tempted to set the whole place on fire. He never wanted to think of Naděžda trapped there, at the mercy of some lecherous, evil man, ever again. As she opened her mouth again, no doubt to argue with him once more, Amir shook his head.

"Not now, Naděžda. I will see to it that Harshad sends someone else," he said. "Right now, I do not care about anything but you."

THE ORDER OF THE CRYSTAL DAGGERS

7

◊

Amir barely realized how much his body ached as he carried Naděžda toward the *Splendor*. He moved quickly through the port, never meeting any individual gaze, remaining focused only on getting her to a place where he could properly care for her wounds. She clung to him as he carried her, and while he reveled in the warmth of her embrace, as necessary as it was, he could feel the warmth of her blood as it oozed through his tunic.

"Amir." Her voice was a whisper as she shivered.

"Not now. We're almost to the ship."

"I can walk."

"I can carry you."

"I'm heavier than I look."

"I'm stronger than I look." He tried to give her a stern look, but his heart softened to the point of aching as he looked down at her. Her eyes were blotchy, shimmering with unshed tears. "I can carry you. So I will."

"I deserve to suffer."

Amir shifted her in his arms, bringing her further up on his chest as her legs fell back over his arm. "If you suffer, I will only suffer more."

"It was my fault they found me. It's my fault we failed in our mission."

"No," Amir whispered back. "I found out where the shipment went, and I know that the perpetrators were warned the Order was supposed to interfere."

56

"That's true." Naděžda gave a ladylike snort. "The men said they recognized my name from when I was talking to the ambassador. That was why I went with them at first."

Amir knew he have easily told her he had been right, but he would never be so wrong in all his life if he dared. Instead, he stopped walking and hugged her closer to him, careful not to rub up against her cuts. "Let's not talk about it anymore. You're safe now. That's what matters."

"I wish you would be upset with me. I ruined the mission, after all."

"And I saved it," Amir told her. He adjusted his grip on her again, before he resumed his trek toward the *Splendor.* "Just like I saved you."

Naděžda gave him a small smile. "Yes. Yes, you did." She reached up and touched his cheek, before tucking her face into the nook of his shoulder.

Amir cradled her head, his fingers lightly caressing her hair.

Despite his aching muscles, it was too soon before the *Splendor* came into sight. The sun was close to setting as Amir carried Naděžda up the gangplank.

As if he'd suspected something had gone wrong, Harshad was waiting for them. Amir did not know if he was more glad or anxious to see his mentor and patron. He did not want to distress Harshad, and he did not want to disappoint Lady Penelope. Amir also did not want to get Naděžda in trouble. Even though he was certain she would be fine, after everything that happened, he only wanted her to rest.

"My goodness, Dezda," Harshad said. His hair seemed to turn grayer as he saw her state of undress and the blood on the back of Amir's tunic. "What happened?"

Amir quickly stepped forward. Harshad listened to Amir as he spoke quickly regarding the day's adventures, briefly mentioning the Bohemian loyalists and the French ambassador's men, before informing him that the *Chaos* was carrying the missing weapons.

"Miss Eleanor has a few injuries, Mr. Prasad," Amir said dutifully. Naděžda's formal name sounded strange to his ears now; he hoped Harshad would not notice. Amir bowed his head down in both greeting and deference, as he hurried to excuse himself. "I request you allow me to see to her care."

"My God." Harshad's graying hair tussled in the salty wind as he studied Naděžda. Amir could see his ochre face blanch at the sight of her blood.

"Oh, Uncle, you needn't worry," Naděžda said with a sigh.

"Your mother will be worried when she gets back from her own meeting with the Chinese ambassadors," Harshad said.

Naděžda delicately wrinkled her nose. "Amir will take excellent care of me, just as he has so far. Mother does not need to worry about that."

Amir was gratified to see her smile in admiration as she looked at him. He had to wonder if she was being sincere, considering she would not want to put in a bad report with Harshad and her mother, either.

Harshad nodded curtly. "Take her to her room," he instructed Amir. "I will see to it that you are not disturbed."

"Thank you, Mr. Prasad," Amir replied.

"Wait." Harshad pausing, before he rubbed his chin. "Perhaps it is time for you to call me 'Harshad,' Amir. As Dezda will tell you, we are very informal with those we consider family."

"Yes, Uncle," Naděžda agreed.

"Thank you," Amir said quietly.

Harshad clasped his hands together, in a gesture of respect. "You have been working with us directly these past few months, and of course, you have known us for many years now. Surely that is enough to know your place is with us."

Amir nodded. "Yes, sir ... Harshad."

"I will check in with you in a few hours, Amir. We have reports to discuss."

"Thank you." Amir quickly bowed and hurried down the deck to where Naděžda's room was located.

"It seems my mother has softened him, since they reunited," Naděžda murmured. "If that is one good thing to come out of my parents' failure of a relationship, it is Uncle."

"I'm surprised your mother could soften anyone," Amir replied, glad to see Naděžda already seemed to be recovering from the trauma of the day. When she chuckled at his comment, he was even more gratified.

Once Naděžda was settled on her bed, Amir got out his small medical kit, the one he carried with him. As he pulled out the items he needed for lacerations, she tried to make small talk with him.

He barely listened to her as he laid her across his lap, as he carefully cut and peeled off the blood-covered tunic he had used to cover her. He set about cleaning off the skin of her back, glad to see that there was only one major wound, a crude lash across her right shoulder blade. Amir could already hear Lady Penelope telling her Socialite friends how Naděžda chaffed herself on passing carriage, as she hurried to save a stray child, or some grand fabrication that would change the scar from a battle wound into a badge of valor.

She might save herself the trouble and allow Naděžda to wear more modest gowns. Even as he thought it, Amir allowed himself a moment to study Naděžda. Even with the injuries interrupting the perfect smoothness of her back, her muscles

59

were strong but subtle; her skin looked infinitely soft, begging for a touch.

Amir had a feeling Lady Penelope would eschew the more modest dresses. Naděžda was a wonder to work with in Society. Her charm and beauty easily made others believe her various backstories, allowing the Order to discover even the most carefully guarded secrets Society tried to hide.

Amir did his best to treat her as if she were any patient in the world, but as he stitched up the slash in her back from the foreman's whip, he had to pause several times because of his own trembling hands.

I almost lost her.

Naděžda shifted beneath him. "Amir?"

"Yes?" His tongue suddenly felt very thick.

"Are you feeling well?"

He hated lying to her, especially since he had a feeling she would know he was. "I am perfectly capable of doing my job, if you are worried about that."

"I wasn't," she replied. "I was more worried because I saw you kill the foreman. I know you very well, and such an action is contrary to your nature."

He said nothing. He only continued to thread his medical needle through the skin on her back, carefully tugging on the threat.

"I'm right, aren't I?" She glanced back at him, carefully shifting her hair behind her.

"You need to lie still," he said instead. "I only have a few stitches left."

"Amir."

THE ORDER OF THE CRYSTAL DAGGERS

"You likely don't want any worse of a scar," Amir said. "Please, hold still. For just a few moments longer."

She acquiesced, but the moment he snipped the thread and tied it off, she pushed herself up and reached for him. The gesture was so natural and smooth he never stopped to wonder or question her.

"I'm sorry you had to kill someone in order to protect me," she whispered.

"He hurt you." Amir's arms involuntarily tightened around her.

He could feel her smile into his shoulder. "Are you worried Uncle and my mother will punish you for what happened?"

Amir sighed. He did not like to think of their earlier argument. "No, Miss Eleanor."

"Stop that." Naděžda, sensing she had overstepped the limits of his patience. "I know what you're trying to do, and it won't work. I know you want to call me Naděžda, Amir. I know it, just as you surely know how much I want you to."

He said nothing, but his heart began to race. The thundering beat was pounding into him as Naděžda buried her face further into his shoulder.

"I hate this, you know," she whispered quietly, as though she was tearing the words from the deepest part of her heart, the part she never admitted aloud to anyone, possibly not even herself. Her eyes watered as she looked up at him. "I hate this life, Amir. I hate feeling like there is no true place I belong, that there is no true family for me."

"You have your mother and Mr. Prasad," Amir reminded her, tucking her hair back with one hand while wiping away a stray tear with his thumb. He caressed her cheek, reveling in the softness of her skin. Despite her toughness, she seemed so delicate to the touch.

61

She deserved so much more than what life had offered her, he thought.

"It's not enough," she choked out, twisting his shirt into her fingers. "I want my own family. I want my own life. I want to be free—free from my mother's expectations, and free from the Order."

Amir drew her against his chest again. He let her cry, knowing there was nothing he could say to her to make it better.

In some ways, he wished he could cry with her. Who, more than he, knew the honor required to follow a parents' wishes, even if it meant great cost? And who could know the horror of failing to live up to those expectations more than he did?

He had killed a man, even though it was to protect an innocent woman, and he worked in service to a woman, even if it was profitable.

He had fallen in love with a spy, the illegitimate daughter of his employer, a woman his family would never accept. It was all folly, all of it; there was too much keeping them apart— religion, culture, bloodlines, status, and the honor he had always striven to achieve.

"You have me, too," he whispered.

"I do?"

"Yes." He looked into her eyes and lost himself all over again, Amir knew it was more possible to stop the sun from shining than it was to stop himself from loving her. "Yes, of course you do ... Naděžda."

Before the last echo of her name had begun to fade between then, Naděžda's arms were laced around his neck, her body was pressed up hard against his, and all the illusions between them were gone. All other choices between them were gone. All pretense, all innocence, all hope of any other life—no matter how orderly and neat and uncomplicated as it might have been—all of it had passed away, and only need remained.

"Amir." His name was a breath on her lips, a second before his lips were on hers.

The taste of her rushed at him and through him, penetrating into his core as she kissed him. The warm spice of her mouth, mixed with the wetness of her bitter tears, sent tremors through him, shaking his soul even as his heart reveled in the sudden security of knowing she was his, and he was hers.

No matter how much he might have imagined it, kissing Naděžda was beyond anything he'd ever experienced; it was both beyond sin and forgiveness, beyond memory and dreams. Passion, ardent and pervasive, coursed through him like fire on a fuse; the taste of her drove deeply into him, penetrating past all possible defenses, confirming his transgression even as it tasted of divine ecstasy.

Her mouth opened under his, and his body promptly rejected every last ounce of self-control he had built up over the last several months since Naděžda had become his constant companion. All he lived for in that moment was to drown in her.

"Amir." His name escaped from her in a moan before she eased back, breathing heavily. "I have been trying so hard, you know, to get you to fall in love with me. Perhaps it was foolish of me."

"Yes." Amir brushed a stray lock of hair away from her face as he looked down at her. "It was."

"Well, if that's how you feel—" Naděžda began to push away from him, but Amir only pulled her close and kissed her again.

THE ORDER OF THE CRYSTAL DAGGERS

"Naděžda," he whispered. "I have been falling in love with you from the first moment we met."

"Oh." A lovely, shocked expression of wonder lit up her face as she relaxed into him again.

"Are you finally speechless?" Amir shook his head. The muscles in his face seemed to crack as he smiled. "I should have told you sooner."

"It might have saved us several arguments." Naděžda gave him a small smile, both shy and sly as she looked up at him. "I hope you don't think this is how you'll win in the future."

"I guess we'll see."

"Amir." Naděžda's hands slid under his shirt, grasping at his shoulders as they fell back together.

Amir fell into her kiss, devastatingly overwhelmed and overly eager to claim her. Over and over their lips met in a fierce fire, his soul suturing itself into hers as he tasted and touched her. He could feel her own eagerness as her hands ran down his chest, as her kisses offered silent confessions and hinted at the desperate desires of her heart.

Amir let his hands fall to her hips, letting his hands run down her corset and his fingers fold into the ties of her pantalettes. Nothing was able to stop him from seeking out the warmth of her skin; her being called out to his, and he was just as desperate as she was to burn.

It was only when she lifted herself off his chest, pausing as she panted for breath, that he saw her apprehension.

"What is it, Naděžda? Are you afraid I will resort to my mongrel ways?" he whispered teasingly, before letting his lips linger against her temple.

"I am not afraid of you." While her words were sure, there was a new edge in her voice that told him there was something making her hesitate.

"What is it then?"

He almost did not want to know. While it seemed like a miracle that Naděžda loved him at all, there were still so many things that would keep them apart. He watched as Naděžda fidgeted with the collar of his shirt, and he mentally prepared for her list of possible objections.

He already knew them, of course. There was the issue of her mother; Amir inwardly groaned at the thought of telling Lady Penelope he wanted Naděžda for himself. She would not accept him. She saw him as an acquaintance, a necessary member of their small team of trusted people. He was breaching that trust in itself by confessing his love to Naděžda. There was no telling how much he would destroy the rest of that trust, should they act on their love.

And then there was the Order itself as well. Could they be together with the business of the Order between them? And what about a family? Was it possible they could have children and raise them, with their lives' chosen work at risk? The Order did necessary work to keep the different corners of the world from warring with each other, even if it was distasteful and improper at times.

Amir felt his hope shrink as Naděžda finally met his eyes with hers again.

"Will I always be your only love, Amir?"

The question took him by surprise. "What are you talking about?" he asked. "There is no one but you."

"Truly?" She pressed her forehead against his. "I know things are different for us when it comes to matters like love and marriage, but I ... I've never ... "

For the first time in all the years he'd known her, Naděžda genuinely blushed, and Amir was touched to see it was not the small, flirtatious flush he'd seen on her cheeks many times as they interviewed informants or possible targets. Her face burned crimson all over, no longer full of shallow charm but something more than serious.

"I know that love and marriage is different in the East," she said, trying again. "I know you grew up where you can have up to four wives and any number of lovers, but—"

"You are the only one I want." He kissed her throat, enjoying how she shivered against him at the intimate caress. "You are the only one I've ever wanted, and you are the only one I will ever want. I promise."

"You do?"

"I do." He looked into her wide eyes, searching for any sign of uncertainty in her gaze, determined to scourge it from her heart and soothe any more of her silent fears. "And if anything, Eastern marriage is easier. All we have to do is sign a contract, one only between ourselves."

"No archbishop required?"

He smiled. "No."

Her eyes filled with sudden worry, and he wondered if she was thinking of her mother or the Order; she could have been wondering about the Islamic traditions of marriage, if any contract between them would hold up in the Catholic church. He reached up and cupped her chin, running his thumb over the softness of her cheek once more.

"I love you," he whispered. "Let me love you, Nadĕžda, as long as life allows me. Please."

"I've never loved anyone the way I love you." She hesitated for only the slightest half-second longer before she curled into his embrace, all tension gone. "I trust you, Amir."

Amir stared at her mouth, stricken. Her words were soft, laced with an intimacy he knew she had never shared with anyone else.

THE ORDER OF THE CRYSTAL DAGGERS

Later on, and multiple times, Amir would think about how he should have pushed her away—how he should have promised her the wedding he wanted to give her, how he should have done something besides sit there and embrace his doom with such self-destructive relish.

How they should have talked about leaving the Order.

How they should have talked about their future with a family.

How they should have done anything but choose to throw their fate into passion's perilous winds.

But before Amir could say or do anything else, Naděžda leaned over and kissed him again, moving her body against his, pushing back all barriers between them. Amir groaned as he felt the last of his restraint crumble inside of him; he could not stop himself from choosing her, even if it was reckless, even if it was all folly.

The last thing he heard himself say as he gave himself over to the darkness and light of her love was her name.

"Naděžda."

THE ORDER OF THE CRYSTAL DAGGERS

C. S. Johnson is an award-winning, genre-hopping author of several novels, including *The Starlight Chronicles* series, the *Once Upon a Princess* saga, and the *Divine Space Pirates* trilogy. With a gift for sarcasm and an apologetic heart, she currently lives in Atlanta with her family.

THE ORDER OF THE CRYSTAL DAGGERS

AUTHOR'S NOTE

Dear Reader,

As always, I am deeply indebted to the people who spend their time inside my work, and I think this story in particular is a sign of your dedication. For those of you who are reading this because of *Kingdom of Ash and Soot* or the other books from The Order of the Crystal Daggers, you likely know most of what happens to Amir and Naděžda—and all the others who get name-dropped and cameos in here—after this.

Amir and Naděžda's story is a tragic tale, one of so many boundaries and barricades that it is almost more painful to know that while they manage to overcome all of them, it is only for a short time.

Can there be beauty despite an unhappy ending? Or can the tragedy enhance the beauty found within the brokenness?

That's one of those tricky questions we can ask ourselves about life, and it's never an easy one to tackle. Can there be good that shines through the overwhelmingly bad?

While I was writing this novel, the idea that kept coming into my head was the story of Hudson Taylor. For those of you who know me so well, Taylor's story is a large part of the reason I became a Christian. At the young age of seven, I went to my Good News Club during the summer—which, lucky for me, was held in my own basement—and I heard Taylor's tale. He was a missionary in the 1800s who went to China to spread the gospel. Once he got there, he began to realize the people there did not understand him. So he let his skin grow dark, he dyed his hair, he learned the language of the Chinese, and he wore their clothes. He did everything he could to earn the people's trust and communicate the gospel.

I remember that day and that story so clearly. I remember thinking of all the things he did, and how Jesus did even more to find a way to communicate God's truth. Jesus came to this world wrapped in the flesh of a human, donning the lungs and eyes and heart of man, putting on hair—even armpit hair, and likely a beard—he learned to speak our language, he wore the clothes spun from wool and wore the sandals made by human hands. Taylor could have lived a far more comfortable life in Europe, and Jesus did not have to come down to this world from Heaven.

This, to me, at a young age of seven, was truly life-changing, and I remember asking Jesus to come and live in my heart that day. I even remember feeling the rush of wind inside of me as I did, and I distinctively remember this because I tried asking him a second time and nothing happened.

And now, more than two decades of backsliding and rededication and doubting and wrestling and learning later, I sit here, typing out the question that's most likely on your mind: What does this have to do with this story?

It turns out that there is much more to the story of Hudson Taylor, which I did not learn until nearly a year ago. Taylor was faithful as a missionary for many years, but at the end of his life, he fell into a deep depression, noting that he was even too depressed to pray. He died very quietly, and no one thought to highlight the very anti-climactic and somewhat depressing last days of his life.

Despite all the years of service and winning souls through his work, he still experienced depression's depths—depths I am more familiar with than I would like—and so great was his despair that he seemed to have given up.

Does this mean my own life is destined to end in despair, too? Am I wasting my life on something that is largely wind and shadow to this world?

Uncomfortable questions, for sure, and those are only followed by more.

Is there still redemption and hope for Hudson Taylor, in light of the great darkness he faced at the end? Is there some beauty for Amir and Naděžda, although they were tragically parted and their love was left largely unresolved?

THE ORDER OF THE CRYSTAL DAGGERS

I like to think so. And not just because I am a hopeless romantic, but also because I am a hopeful believer.

God might be the god of irony to me, the god of laughter and cunning, but I also see him as the Grand Storyteller, and I know from my own life story that he is able to redeem my darkest moments and use them to shed light on others' lives. Time and time again, I have seen the restoration, the reclamation that God does to his children's lives, and I am encouraged to think that where emptiness now lies, one day it will be overflowing with revealed beauty.

That does not mean those painful moments means permanent breaks, that those difficult situations become magically easy to bear. "Beauty" is not always synonymous with "happy," and perhaps that is the greatest discomfort we must face as humans fallen under time's power.

I am sure you will find similar questions and similar themes in my other work—such as in my novella, *The Princess and the Peacock*. There is a sample following this note, and I hope you will read on to see it.

It is always a beautiful thing for me, to see familiar readers looking forward to finding another piece of my heart.

Until We Meet Again,

C. S. Johnson

THE ORDER OF THE CRYSTAL DAGGERS

AUTHOR'S ACKNOWLEDGEMENTS

EDITOR

Jennifer C. Sell

 Jennifer Clark Sell is a professional book editor and proofreader. She works from her home in Southern California. With her years of professional and personal experience, she offers several quality packages for authors. Find her at

https://www.facebook.com/JenniferSellEditingService.

Photo Credit: Savannah Sell

SAMPLE READING

Chapter 1 *from*

THE

Princess

AND THE

Peacock

BIRDS OF FAE

BOOK 1

◊   ◊   ◊   ◊

C. S. Johnson

73

THE ORDER OF THE CRYSTAL DAGGERS

1

◊

The first time I fell in love with Princess Mele was when I saw her smile, and I fell in love with her the second time the moment I heard her sing.

The memory of the day I met her is burned into my mind as much as the scars of my mother's death have been scorched on my hands—my hands, which are currently full of cuts and scrapes as I make my way up the Forbidden Mountain.

Its steep climb and deep crevices make for easier climbing than it first appears, but there have been enough deaths in my village that no one has tried to climb it for several summers now. The last warrior to go up the mountain was during the summer of my seventeenth year. After he fell, he was left to die at the foot of the mountain, his body broken and his eyes blinded.

I know all of this because I am the one who found him, and Appa was the one who took him in and nursed him back to health.

The man was saved from death, but not from disgrace. It was thought to be bad luck to touch a blind man in my village. His family reluctantly took him in, and they had been relived he died shortly after, no matter how glorious of a warrior he had once been.

No one wants to care for an outcast.

My eyes fall to my scars on my hands, the ones that wind their way up the left side of my body, curving all around my arms, and dipping down across my back.

No one wants to be associated with one, either.

I know that truth as much as I know the pain associated with my own dismissal from the ranks of my fellow warriors after my disfigurement.

My fingers slip on a rock as it breaks free from the rest of the mountain. I hurry, reaching for another one before I lose my grip completely. I clasp onto another divot in the mountain and slowly release my breath in staggered pants. Even if I am no longer a soldier for my kingdom, and I lost some of my stamina since my mother's death, I still have plenty of strength from my years of training.

The blood on my palms is sticky and hot, compelling me onward and upward, but I know I should take a moment to rest, to allow my heart to slowly beat back to its normal pattern.

Resting does not appeal to me, even though I have been climbing for hours now; I do not want the opportunity to focus on my pain, nor do I want to dwell on the ugliness that brands me as an outcast in my village. I only want to remember the moment Princess Mele entered my world. She came into my world, offering it the only possible hope for meaning and giving me the only reason I had to move forward with my life after the death of my mother.

It might have been two years since I fell in love with her, but not a night has gone by since that I do not dream of her. And now that King Ahanu, her father, is ready to see her wed, I have to do something quickly if I was to earn her hand in marriage.

So I need to do this, I tell myself. No matter how hard it is, I need to climb up the Forbidden Mountain.

Remembering her beauty is the only way I will make it to the top of the mountain, the only way I can ever hope to gain beauty of my own. And that means forgetting my pain, no matter how well I am accustomed to it.

75

THE ORDER OF THE CRYSTAL DAGGERS

"Kaipo, wait up."

As I hear my name, I groan and nearly stumble again.

Rahj is calling for me.

As I struggle to secure myself once more, I am torn between irritation and relief. I pull back from the mountain, very, very carefully, enough to where I can peek through the crook by elbow. More than twenty *guz* below me, my best and only friend is faithfully following me.

Reluctantly, I settle further into the mountain crevice where I've stopped, deciding it is better for Rahj to catch up to me.

That was the big secret of success when it comes to climbing the Forbidden Mountain—it was much easier to climb if someone else was around to help. No one else seemed to realize this.

But then, there was a reward at stake. If a climber wanted to earn a wish from Jaya, the Fae Queen residing at the peak, he had to survive the climb to see her. In all the centuries since our kingdom's founders settled on the isle of Maluhia, only a few warriors have ever completed the task.

I look up, squinting past the longer strands of my ash brown hair to gaze at the majestic mountain as its peak disappears into the lofty clouds. Even on clear days, no one ever sees the crown of the mountain; it is well-known that Jaya likes her privacy, and with all her birds and magic for company, she never willingly bothers the mortals residing on her island.

"I'm coming, Kaipo. You sure are a fast climber!" The chill in the high mountain allows his voice to move more swiftly through the air between us.

I watch as Rahj draws closer to me. Out of the corner of my eye, I can see the tunic Rahj is wearing; it is one of my older ones, one of the few we had been able to save from the fire. It strikes a stark contrast with the brightness around it, but the charcoal dye

THE ORDER OF THE CRYSTAL DAGGERS

manages to hide a good deal of tears and dirt. My own tunic is better repaired, but the lighter tan coloring brings out the whiteness of my scars.

I lean back and look over at him as he climbs up beside me. "Are you doing well, Rahj?" I ask, already knowing the answer he will give.

Rahj comes up beside me, the usual grin on his face. "Of course I am well, brother."

I never know why he is so happy. I try not to let his persistent cheerfulness bother me as we continue our climb up the mountain.

I used to hate Rahj, and I remember this on occasions such as this one. It has been seven years since he came to live with us after Appa saved his life.

To this day, I do not know the full story of how it happened; I only knew Rahj was a former child slave from the neighboring island of Aruna, one of the of many boys castrated in service to the temple goddesses. My father went to Aruna in hopes of trading some of his herbal mixtures for some new supplies for us.

But instead of new tools or perhaps even some of the exotic candies from the West my friends' fathers purchased, my father bought Rahj, using all his coins and trading the last of his medicines to do so.

It seemed my father's action would doom us all, especially when Appa told us he'd brought Rahj home to live with us, not as a slave, but as an adopted son. Several members of my family, including my mother, grew suspicious of the strange boy suddenly part of our family; with his ochre skin and his reddish hair, many assumed Rahj was my father's bastard, born to him by an Arunian temple prostitute.

The whispers only got worse as my mother rejected my father and refused to see him again so long as he was alive.

THE ORDER OF THE CRYSTAL DAGGERS

From that day on, my mother took to her bed, always insisting she was ill. When I asked her about it, as young as I was, she insisted that something had to be wrong with her, that she had only been able to have one son, and that Appa still felt the need to buy his own.

"Something is probably wrong with you, too, Kaipo," she muttered, before shoving me away and pulling her blanket over her head. I never saw her move from her bed after that, not even when Appa died, just shy of my eighteenth year.

At the thought of my mother, seeing her sad and crying as she burned herself to death, I look down at my hands. They are currently full of blood and dirt, the stinging mixture serving as an adhesive between me and the side of the mountain I was climbing.

The pain I'd pushed back earlier refuses to be ignored any longer. The vicious rawness courses through my body, roaming from the tips of my bloody fingers to the center of my heart, before flying up and anchoring itself into my mind. The alarm I feel sends tremors down my body, and I squeeze my eyes shut and force myself to keep going.

The rocks continue to rip into my palms as I climb, but I use the thought of Princess Mele to ward off the pain, just like I used to keep her memory close at night, when I would worry bad dreams would come to me after my mother died.

One side of my mouth quirks up in an involuntary smile; the idea of remaining calm while hanging onto the side of a mountain—let alone the Forbidden Mountain, the home of the Fae Queen, Jaya— is laughable.

"Hey, Kaipo, we are almost at the top!" Rahj lets out a cheer as he appears beside me again. He daringly loosens his grip before twisting around to see the sights behind us. "Can you believe the view from up here? No wonder Jaya chose to live here."

THE ORDER OF THE CRYSTAL DAGGERS

I carefully look down at the view below. I can see our whole side of Maluhia as I glance around us. The skies are clear, shining in a way that seems both too light and too blue; the clouds just above the Forbidden Mountain are fluffy and starkly white, as if they know they are used in service to a higher power.

The seas that surround Maluhia are a mix of blue and green, as if the sun and sky eagerly battled for the right to blend their beauty. I can see the coral reef that bends around the beach that leads to the other side of the mountain, where the kingdom's rich merchants, warriors, and royal family live in the capital city of Shanthi.

"You're right," I say to Rahj, who somehow smiles even more brightly. "This is incredible."

"This is how the God of all creation must see the world," Rahj says, his voice full of awe. "From up here, it only looks beautiful. There is no way to see the full ugliness the world carries."

I frown at him, surprised by the remark. There was nothing in his tone to suggest a sullen feeling, but the words were enough to make me wonder.

"I am happy to share this with you, Kaipo." Despite the danger, Rahj reaches out and I clasp his hand in mine.

I might have hated Rahj before, but since my scars had branded me as both an outcast and an orphan, he had remained by my side. With Appa gone, and my mother dead and burned, there was no one else.

So I smile at him. "Thank you, brother," I reply, and this time, Rahj does not smile. Instead, I can see the solemn gratitude and pride in his gaze as he nods.

His sudden and uncharacteristic seriousness is the last thing I see before the rock under his anchored hand crumbles, and he cries out my name as he falls.

"Kaipo!"

THE ORDER OF THE CRYSTAL DAGGERS

THE ORDER OF THE CRYSTAL DAGGERS

Thank you for reading! Please leave a review for this book and check out www.csjohnson.me for other books and updates!

THE ORDER OF THE CRYSTAL DAGGERS

THE ORDER OF THE CRYSTAL DAGGERS

CPSIA information can be obtained
at www.ICGtesting.com
Printed in the USA
BVHW031235300520
580600BV00004B/31